# Here Are My Hands

By Bill Martin Jr. and John Archambault
Illustrated by Ted Rand

To Gloria, Theresa, and Martin.
From my hands to your hands.
T.R.

First published in book form in the USA 1987
by Henry Holt & Company, Inc
Published in Picture Lions 1988

Picture Lions is an imprint of the Children's Division,
part of the Collins Publishing Group
8 Grafton Street, London W1X 3LA

Text copyright © 1985 by Bill Martin Jr and John Archambault
Illustrations copyright © 1987 by Ted Rand

Printed by Warners of Bourne and London

# Here Are My Hands

By Bill Martin Jr. and John Archambault
Illustrated by Ted Rand

COLLINS
PICTURE LIONS

Here are my hands
for catching and throwing.

Here are my feet
for stopping and going.

Here is my head

for thinking and knowing.

Here is my nose
for smelling and blowing.

Here are my eyes

for seeing and crying.

Here are my ears
for washing and drying.

Here are my knees
for falling down.

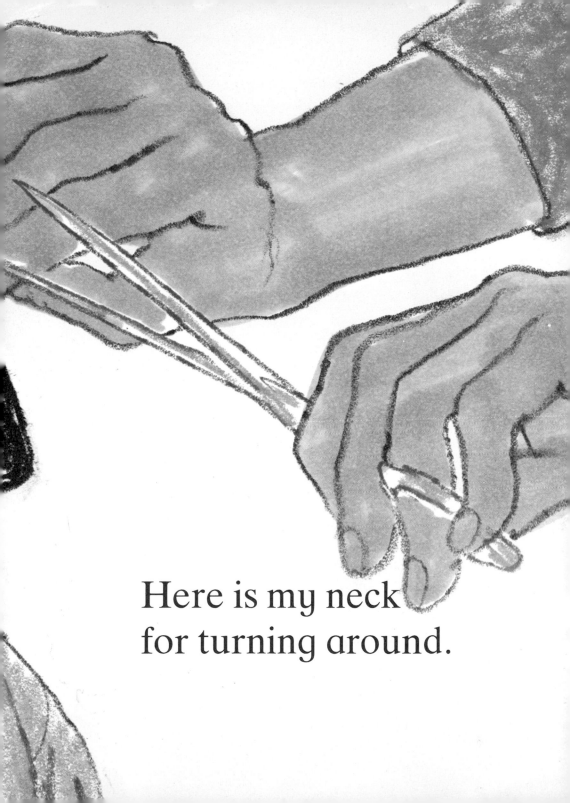

Here is my neck
for turning around.

Here are my cheeks
for kissing and blushing.

Here are my teeth

for chewing and brushing.

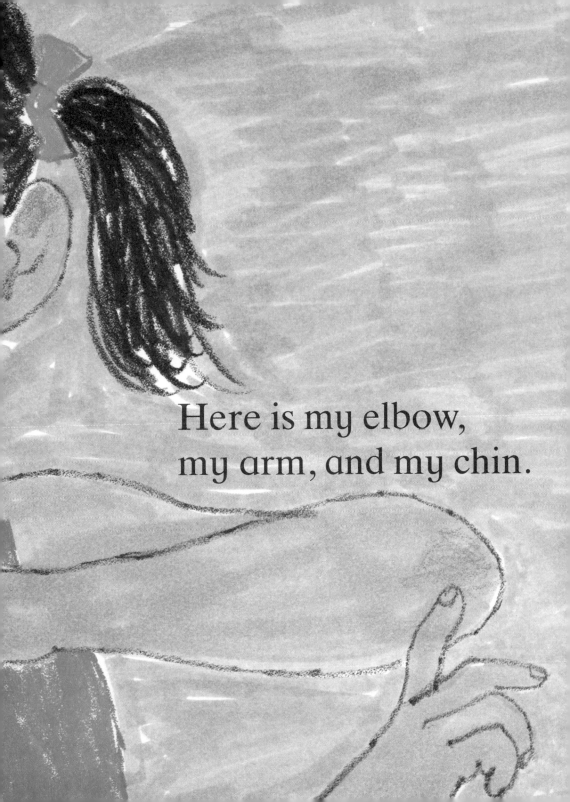

Here is my elbow,
my arm, and my chin.

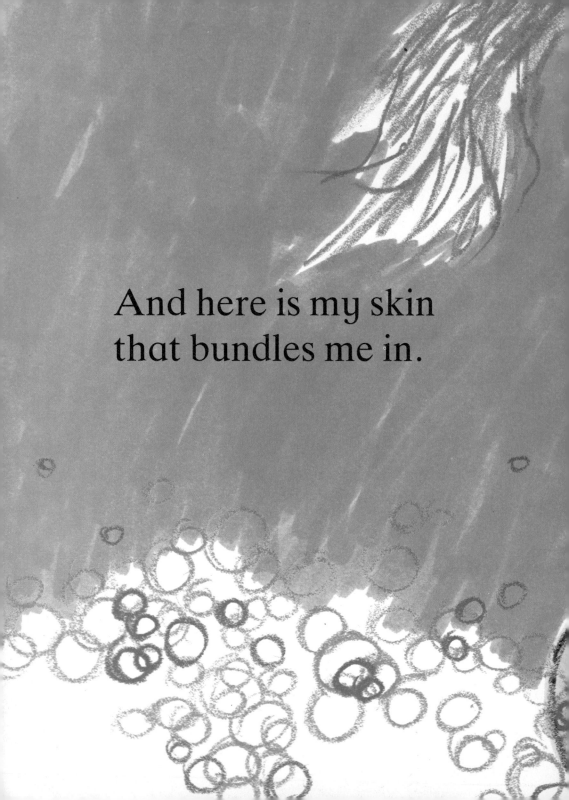

And here is my skin
that bundles me in.

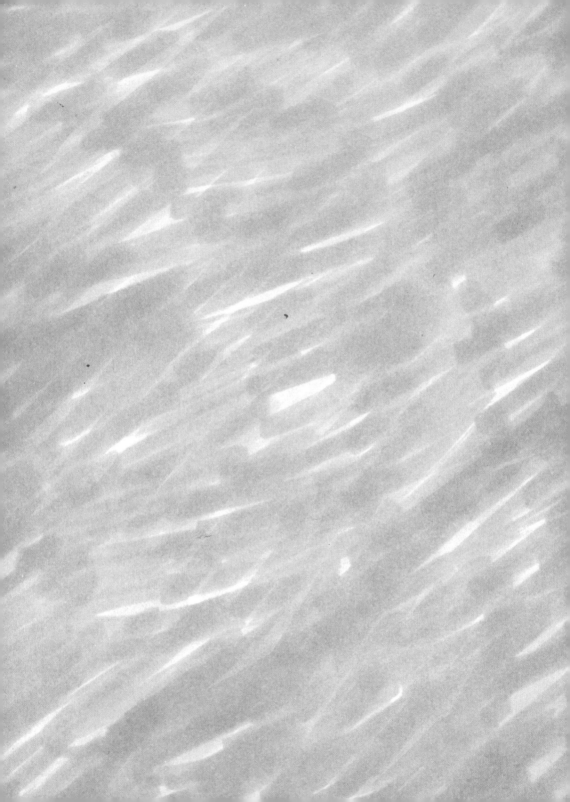